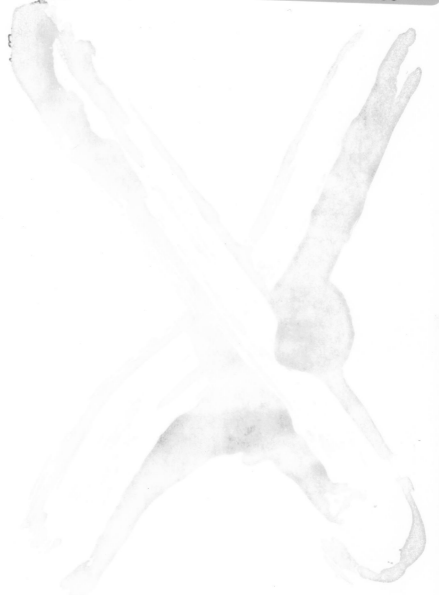

Fierce John

William Pène du Bois

FIERCE JOHN   FIERCE JOHN

for FIERCE LIONS everywhere

FIERCE JOHN

FIERCE JOHN

a story by EDWARD FENTON

illustrated by WILLIAM PÈNE DU BOIS

Holt, Rinehart and Winston   New York Chicago San Francisco

Fierce John

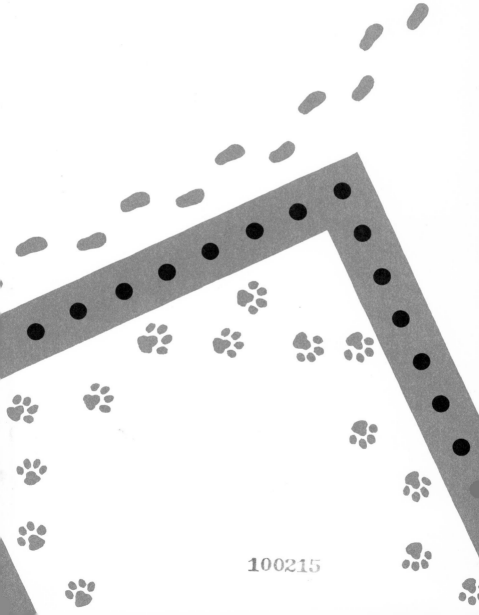

William Pène du Bois

One day John went to the zoo.
He saw all the animals at the zoo.
He gave candy to the bear.
The bear took the candy and ate it.
He gave a nut to the elephant.
The elephant took the nut with its
trunk and ate it.

But the lion did not eat candy.
And the lion did not want a nut.

The lion just looked fierce and roared.

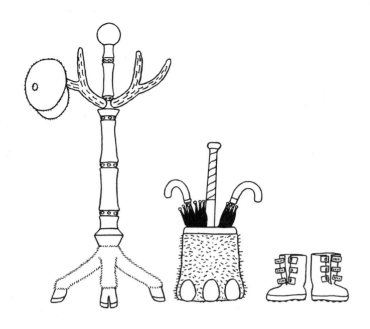

When John came home from the zoo
he said:
"I am not a boy now.
I am an animal.
I am a big fierce animal from the
zoo.
I am a lion!
Now I will roar."
And John roared and looked fierce.

14

"My!" said John's mother.
"What a noise!"

"That noise is me," said John.
"I am very fierce. Are you afraid?"

"No," said his mother.

"I am not afraid of you."

"Why not?" asked John.

"I am busy right now," said his mother.

"Here is some candy.

Now go and play."

"Lions don't eat candy," John said, and went away.

He went to his grandmother's room.
"Hello, John," his grandmother said.
John just roared and looked fierce.

"Must you speak so loud?" said his grandmother. "I can hear you very well.
There are some nuts on the table. You may take some."
"Lions don't eat nuts," John said, and went away.

John met his big brother.
His big brother had a ball and
a bat.
"Hello, John," said his big brother.
John just roared and looked fierce.
"Oh well," said his big brother,
"I don't have any time for baby
games.
I have to go and play ball with
the boys."
John did not say a word.
He roared and looked fierce.
But his brother ran off with his
ball and bat to play with the boys.

22

after John Tenniel

24

John's aunt came along just then.
She heard John roar and saw how
fierce he looked.
"Dear me," said his aunt. "It's John.
Are you sick, dear?"

"Lions are never sick," John said,
and went away.

Soon John's sister came by.
She had her doll with her.
John gave a loud roar and
looked very fierce.

26

"Sh! John," his sister said.
"Go away now. My doll is asleep."
John went away.
He went back inside the house.

He said to himself:
"No one can see that I am a
fierce lion.
And when I roar, they just say
'Go away!'
Or they say, 'Have some candy.'
Or they say, 'Have a nut.'
Or they say, 'Are you sick, dear?'
Everybody knows that lions don't eat
candy.
And lions are never sick.
Lions just roar and look fierce
and make everybody afraid.
But nobody," said John sadly,
"is afraid of me."

Just then John's father came home.

"I will try just one more time,"
said John.
And so just one more time
John roared and looked fierce.

John's father jumped right up on top
of the icebox.
"A lion!" he cried. His voice was
very afraid. "There is a fierce

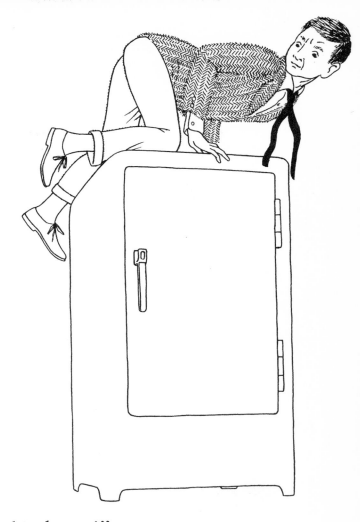

lion in this house!"
John just stood there and roared
very loud and looked even more
fierce than before.

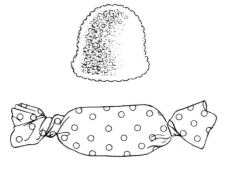

John's mother called,
"What is the matter, dear?"
"There is a lion in the house,"
John's father called back
from the top of the icebox.
"A lion in *our* house?" John's
mother cried.
"Yes," answered John's father.
"And from the look of him,
it is a very fierce lion."
"Dear me," cried John's mother,
and she ran to find a place to hide.
She hid behind a kitchen chair.
John just stood there and roared
and looked fierce.

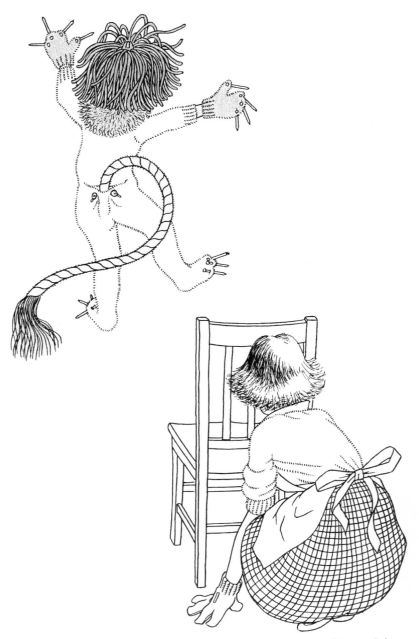

William Pène du Bois

John's grandmother heard all the
noise, so she came out to the kitchen.
"What is going on here?" she said.
"A lion is going on here,"
cried John's mother. "Hide before he
eats you, Grandmother."
"Oh my," said John's grandmother.
"I will stand right here
beside the sink.
Maybe the lion will think I am
a broom."

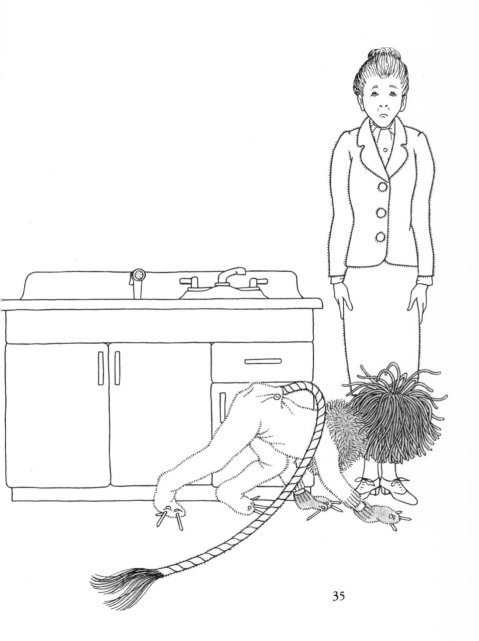

35

Then John's big brother came home
from playing ball.
"Look out!" everybody said.
"A fierce lion from the zoo
is right here in this house."

36

John's big brother did not even wait
to hear the lion roar.
He ran into the yard so fast that
he left his ball and bat behind.

Just then John's aunt came along.
She saw John's father hiding on top
of the icebox.
She saw John's mother hiding behind
a kitchen chair.
She saw John's grandmother right
beside the sink looking like a
broom.
"What is the matter?" said John's
aunt. "Is everybody sick?"
"No," cried John's mother.
"Everybody is afraid.
Hide!
There is a lion in the house!"
John's aunt said,
"I will curl up under the table.

If I hide behind the tablecloth
that lion will never see me."
And so John's aunt curled up under
the table and hid behind the tablecloth.

Soon John's sister came by with
her doll.

Her doll was still asleep.

"Can't you see the lion and hear
it roar?" cried John's father.

"It is a very fierce lion from
the zoo!"

"He will eat my doll if I don't
hide," cried John's sister.

And she climbed on top of the table.

41

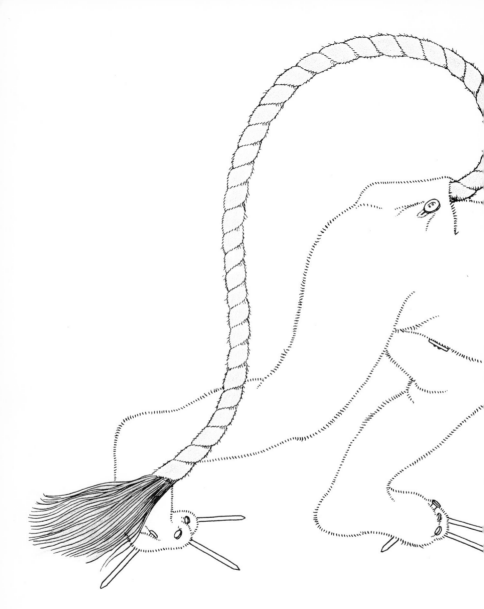

Everyone was hiding.

John was alone in the middle of the
room, roaring and looking fierce.

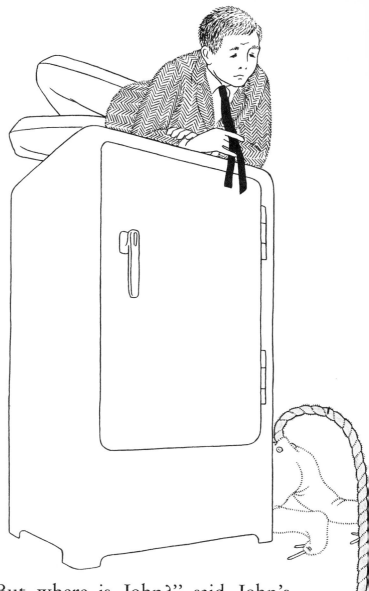

"But where is John?" said John's father from the top of the icebox.

"I think the lion ate John,"
said John's sister from the top
of the table.
"I am sure that the lion will be

sick now," said John's aunt from
under the table.

45

"Poor John!" said John's mother
from behind the chair.
"We will miss him very much."

John's big brother said from the
yard, "I wish I had asked John
to come and play with the boys."

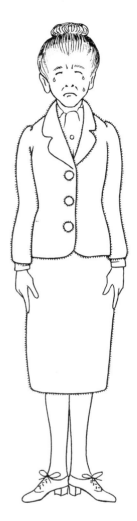

John's grandmother did not say
anything.
She just began to cry.
John felt very sad.

He stopped roaring
and he didn't look fierce any more.
"But I'm John," said John.
"I was John all the time."

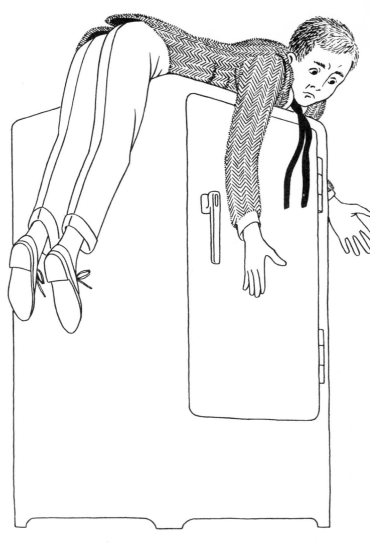

"No you're not," said John's father.
"You're a fierce lion from the zoo,

and you ate my little boy."
"I didn't eat your little boy,"
said John. "I am your little boy."
"My little boy does not roar
and he does not look fierce.
You must be a lion."

"I will show you that I am not
a real lion," said John.

"How?"

asked

everyone

at once.

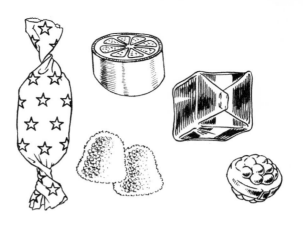

John thought very hard.
"Do you have any candy in the house?"
he asked at last.
"Yes," said John's mother.
"I have some candy."
"If you give me the candy I will
eat it, and then you will know that
I am not a lion, because lions
don't eat candy."
John's mother did not want to
come out from behind the chair.
But she got the candy
and John ate it all.

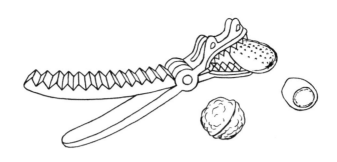

"There," he said.
"Now you know that I am not a lion."
"I am still not sure," said John's
father.
"Maybe you are a bear."
John said:
"Do you have any nuts in the house?
Everyone knows that bears
don't eat nuts."
"Yes, I have some," said John's
grandmother.
And she stopped looking like a broom
and got the nuts from her table.
John ate all the nuts.

"There," he said.
"Now you know that I am not a lion.
And I am not a bear either."
"Maybe you are an elephant,"
said John's father.
John looked very sad.
"But I am John."
"Wait!" said John's mother.
"I know!"
She told John's father to stop
hiding on top of the icebox and
get the ice cream.
"The best way to tell if it is John
and not a lion or a bear or an
elephant is to give him some
ice cream.
John can eat more ice cream than
anyone."
And so they got the ice cream,
and very soon they knew

that it was John after all.